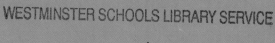

First published 1994 by Pan Macmillan Children's Books

a division of Pan Macmillan Publishers Limited
Cavaye Place London SW10 9PG
and Basingstoke

Associated companies throughout the world

ISBN 0-333-57041-3

1 3 5 7 9 8 6 4 2

A CIP catalogue record for this book is available
from the British Library

Printed in Hong Kong

Sweetie

Jonathan Allen

M

MACMILLAN CHILDREN'S BOOKS

In the great forest lived a family of skunks, Mum, Dad and four young ones. Now, as the forest animals will tell you, skunks make bad smells; that is how they protect themselves. And by "bad smells", the animals don't mean the odd pathetic pong – they mean serious stifling stinks.

Skunks have to practise before they can make smells properly and, in a nearby clearing, the four young skunks were doing just that.

"Get a load of this!" shouted the elder brother.

"Phew, what a whiff!" cried the others.

"If you think that's good," shouted the elder sister, bracing herself, "check this out!"

"Whoooeee! Naff niff of the month!" cried her sister and brothers in admiration.

They took it in turns to try to outwhiff each other, but each time it came to the little sister's turn, try as she might, nothing happened. No whiff, no pong, nothing. The others started to jeer and call her names.

"Go on, Sweetie," they shouted, "waft some whiff!"

"Yeah, Sweetie, ping us a pong!"

So she tried again with all her might and, yes, she made a smell. But it wasn't a nasty smell at all, it was nice! It smelled like spring flowers and green grass. Her sister and brothers fell about laughing.

"What a disgustingly *nice* smell!" cried her big brother.

"What a horribly *pleasant* pong!" shouted her sister.

When her parents heard what had happened, they were
worried.

"It's not right, and it's not natural," they said.

"Skunks are supposed to smell nasty, not go around
smelling of spring flowers and green grass."

The family began to treat Sweetie differently after that.

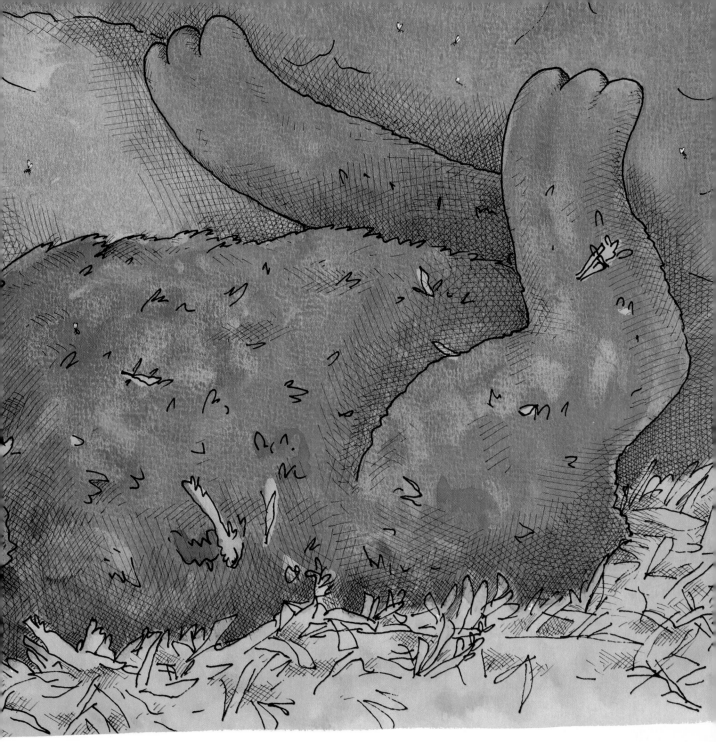

Meanwhile, in a cave not far away, a great big hairy smelly bear was waking up from his winter sleep. He yawned, stretched, and scratched himself. He was filthy, he hadn't washed for years. They didn't call him the Great Big Hairy Smelly Bear for nothing. He sniffed his armpit: it stank.

"Lovely!" he chuckled to himself, grinning.

The skunk family, with Sweetie trailing along behind
them, were walking through the forest looking for food.
Unfortunately, they weren't the only ones feeling hungry. . .
"Yum, yum!" growled the Great Big Hairy Smelly Bear
under his breath as he watched the skunks approaching.

When they were near enough, he leapt out in front of them with a roar.

"*Aahaa!*" he cried. "How nice of you to come to dinner! Or should I say, how nice of you to *become* my dinner!" He laughed nastily and licked his snaggle teeth.

"That's what you think!" cried Sweetie's big brother.
"You're not eating us. Try this for size!"

He leapt forward and let fly with a terrible smell. The
other skunks looked at each other and grinned. They
weren't worried. They knew that as soon as the smell
reached the bear, he would gasp and choke, and then run
away as fast as his legs could carry him.

But he didn't. Instead, he smiled, took a deep breath
and said, "What a lovely smell! It reminds me of my armpit,
only it's not as strong!"

Then he laughed nastily again and leaned forward
towards the now terrified skunks.

"Thank you," he leered, "that's *really* given me an
appetite!"

"This is serious," thought Sweetie. "I must do something!"

Summoning up all her courage, she leapt forward.

"Not so fast, furface!" she cried, defiantly. "Let's see what you make of this!"

So saying, she made the most powerful whiff of her life. But, just as before, it wasn't nasty, it was nice. It smelled of spring flowers and green grass.

Her family hung their heads in despair. It was a brave try, but this was surely the end.

As the smell reached him, the Great Big Hairy Smelly Bear stopped in his tracks.

"Urgle!" he choked, grasping his throat. "Spring flowers! *Eeeuurgh!* Green grass! What horrendously nice smells! How disgustingly fresh and pleasant! *YAAGH!* It reminds me . . . of . . . soap! *AAAGH!* Save me!"

Wailing, gasping, and holding his nose, the Great Big Hairy Smelly Bear ran off as fast as his legs would carry him.

The skunks were overjoyed. They cheered and hugged each other in delight and relief.

"Sweetie! You saved our lives!" they cried. "*And* after we were so nasty to you! Can you ever forgive us?"

"I might," said Sweetie, " if you promise to be *very* nice to me from now on."

"We will," they promised, solemnly.

And they were as good as their word. From that day onwards Sweetie's family treated her with the love and respect she deserved, and the Great Big Hairy Smelly Bear never bothered them again.